Fruit of the Spirit

GALATIANS 5:22-23A

Tabetha McLemore
DeShann Cross Illustrator

WestBow Press books may be ordered through booksellers or by contacting:

WestBow Press
A Division of Thomas Nelson & Zondervan
1663 Liberty Drive
Bloomington, IN 47403
www.westbowpress.com
1 (866) 928-1240

ISBN: 978-1-5127-7196-1 (sc)
ISBN: 978-1-5127-7195-4 (e)

Library of Congress Control Number: 2017900613

Print information available on the last page.

WestBow Press rev. date: 3/27/2017

WESTBOW
PRESS®
A DIVISION OF THOMAS NELSON
& ZONDERVAN

DEDICATION

To the minds and hearts of all humanity. –T.M.

First Presbyterian Kindergarten Terrell (FPK Terrell)
Preschool, Pre-K, and Kindergarten class of 2016. Thank
you for the color scheme on faithfulness! –T.M.

To the present and future generations to come; may these fruit
reside within, and be with you through life's journey. –D.C.

FOREWORD

The Fruit of the Spirit is essential teaching for little ones. It's the character of Christ in a language they can see and understand. Tabetha has captured the heart of these teachings with her vision of childlike faith poured onto these pages for children of all ages to learn and grow. This is the perfect book for parents to introduce God's will for young lives in an inspiring way.

Cathy Lourenco; BS Early Childhood Education

But the fruit of the Spirit is...

Love,

God is Love

Joy,

Peace,

It is more fun when we share!

Patience,

You were right!
The slide was so fast!

Goodness,

Be respectful
Be considerate
No bullying

RULES

Use your walking feet
Use your inside voice
Hands to yourself

Let's do the right thing!
Believe in yourself!
You can do It!

Faithfulness,

Day after day, Year after year

Gentleness,

Mommy says use gentle touches.

I really want a piece of candy,
but mommy and daddy said no.

and Self control,

I am so glad that I listened and obeyed mommy and daddy,
now I can have two pieces of candy tomorrow!

Galatians 5:22-23 "But the fruit of the Spirit is love, joy, peace, patience, kindness, goodness, faithfulness, gentleness, self-control; against such things there is no law."

And these fruit grow in us, as we grow in Jesus :

Love

Joy

Peace

Patience

Kindness

Goodness

Faithfulness

Gentleness

Self control

Just for You

OH LITTLE PRECIOUS ONE

Oh little precious one how do you do?

Jesus gave his life for you: this my **love** is true:

Joy, Peace, and **Patience** shall always be:

Don't forget **Kindness, Goodness,** and **Faithfulness** for these my little one's

you will also see:

Gentleness is great in its very own way:

Self-Control will help you grow from day to day:

Oh little precious one from these fruits you must not part:

Jesus will always keep them close to your precious little hearts.

Author Jacqueline Neal

A SIMPLE PRAYER JUST FOR

_____ (Child's name)

I thank you Lord for today. God is good, God is great.

No matter what my journey brings, by faith I walk in victory.

In Jesus name, Amen.

ABOUT THE AUTHOR

Author Tabetha McLemore is a poet, entrepreneur, and caregiver for medically fragile children. She has worked with medically fragile children in their homes for over 12 years. During this time she discovered that each child had unseen gifts. Many of the children were unable to outwardly express their gifts, but inwardly their luminous gifts shone brightly. Being led through the fruit of the Spirit, Tabetha McLemore cultivated the gifts within these children beyond a caregiver-patient relationship and began to witness the outward expressions of their once dormant potential. Her arduously heartfelt efforts helped each child come closer to achieving their life's greatness. These interactions included reading, singing, and seeing beyond the limitations of their medical diagnosis. Tabetha McLemore's gifts grew through the unveiling of each child's fruit of the Spirit, which prepared the way for her authorship.

CPSIA information can be obtained
at www.ICGtesting.com
Printed in the USA
BVHW052121080519
547776BV00010B/147/P